KUIPER

STATION

Future Chron Universe

Volume 9

From The Earth Series

Book 9

D.W. PATTERSON

Thirteenth Printing – May, 2023

1

Bob James wasn't sure about the meta-verse and being a virtual being, it wasn't that he had doubts about the simulated world designed and engineered by the Artificial General Intelligence's called Aggies, the meta-verse had been around for almost a century and there was no reason to think that it wouldn't continue. And if you considered virtual beings in a simulation as human, then a third of humanity had voluntarily opted for the meta-verse lifestyle.

And it wasn't because, like Bob, they had lived a long life and had no other choice. No, many had chosen the meta-verse early in their lives. According to the research that Bob had done, the meta-verse offered people freedom from aging with the promise of a vastly increased lifespan. Death in the meta-verse, if it ever came, was because it was desired or because something had gone horribly wrong with the supporting hardware. This freedom from aging and the indefinite lifetime it allowed made it possible to be anything a person could imagine, sometimes to good repute, sometimes to bad.

The meta-verse wasn't like physical society, there weren't those that led and those that followed, unless they wanted to lead or follow. Each and everyone could be, if they wished, a separate and sovereign nation. Bit-nations, they were called. Because the meta-verse denizens needed nothing but a tiny amount of electrical power, the give and take of human life as it was experienced in the physical world didn't apply. If there were bad actors in the meta-verse, it was because they wanted to be that way and not because they were trying to alleviate some basic need or want.

The vast meta-verse simulation created by the Aggies was flawless. Even though people could choose to return to their bodies if they didn't wait too long, merging the memories of their time in the meta-verse with old, no one had ever asked for such a thing. Most people communicated from the meta-verse to the physical universe for a short while but it wasn't long until the divergence between the two was too great to bridge and contact was gradually lost.

Still, Bob wasn't sure. Three-hundred and fifty years of life was hard to deny. He was one of those that had never even allowed body implants to enhance his cognition or senses. Now taking on another body, even if just a simulated body, was as frightening to him as anything he had ever done. Still, he had no choice. The life-extension technologies had done as much as they could for him. Biology and physics still imposed a limit on life span and Bob had reached that limit.

He would sleep tonight one last time in his own bed and they would take him tomorrow for the brain scan. Like the others, he could choose to return to his body if the meta-verse wasn't to his liking. But he was pretty sure he wouldn't, he was pretty sure he would be saying goodbye to his old body even if the meta-verse wasn't the paradise he expected.

The body he would leave behind was tired, even past tired, of the struggle to continue in its present form. So it was the meta-verse or oblivion, he thought, as he closed his eyes.

Civilization, like a human body, has an ebb and flow. Society advances in spurts, centuries of quick development, followed by centuries of slow change.

After the Aggie managers took over, technology development exploded. And the effect on human civilization was profound and stultifying, a slow descent into stagnation resulted.

Human initiative, at least where there were Aggie managers, greatly diminished. Most people saw no point in trying to compete with the Aggies. Those still with aspirations migrated to the outer solar system, Saturn's Titan, Neptune's Triton and Uranus Station which were under the auspices of the Solar Federation. Others built space habitats with the capacity to carry thousands, even millions while orbiting the outer planets. These adventurers brought with them what was left of human ambition and the desire for freedom. The Jackson family was among them.

2

Jacob Jackson looked through the small portal of the *Starfisher* into the blackness of space. After four weeks the second-generation fusion-powered spaceship, belonging to the Solar Federation, which had launched from Neptune's orbit was over halfway to its destination. Tharsis was a small body in the Kuiper Belt, named after the Martian volcanic plateau because of its own high plateau region. Tharsis was some 40 AU or 40 times the distance from the sun as the Earth at this time though its orbit was elliptical and could reach out to 70 AU at its most extreme. Jacob and his dad, Jonah Abram Jackson, had campaigned for this mission to be undertaken ever since Jacob was a young man.

The Solar Federation was the outer world's counterweight to the Terran Federation which represented the space ambitions of much of Earth and Mars. Simplistically then, the Solar Federation stood for exploration, the Terran Federation for the consolidation, the Solar Federation for freedom and self-reliance, the Terran Federation for safety and enforced cooperation. The Solar Federation was smaller but more nimble than the Terran Federation and as such was a constant source of irritation to the larger Federation. The Solar Federation preceded the Terran Federation in almost all explorations, even though the Terran Federation had the backing of the Aggies as a powerful resource for technology and organizing society.

Jonah Jackson thought it imperative that exploration, which had been stalled since Jupiter's moon Callisto had been settled by the Solar Federation a century before, be restarted. He wasn't sure what had happened to the human spirit. The development of Artificial General Intelligence and its technological advances had certainly affected that spirit on Earth. And as a direct result, the physical population of Earth had declined. For many years now the adventurous on Earth chose the meta-verse, not the Solar System. Even those left in the physical world were more docile and compliant with a consequent decline in their ambition and drive.

Mars had also "slowed" down in its development. Certainly, the expansion out into the Solar System and especially the abundant resources in the Asteroid Belt had mitigated the drive to explore further for more resources. But there was something else happening, for Mars was a relatively young civilization and with the efficiencies provided by the Aggies it could be expected that the recent settlers of Mars would be quite eager to continue to participate in man's unique destiny in space. But it wasn't so and Jonah had often talked with his son Jacob about why he thought human nature had reached a turning point, at least on Mars and Earth.

"Outwardly," said Jonah to Jacob one evening before the ship left for Tharsis, "people are the same as they've always been, pretty self-centered. The human race has never put much thought into its future as a whole. And most people haven't thought very far ahead in their personal lives either. But something else has changed since the Aggies and their life-extending technologies arrived. You know that life expectancy has recently been increasing at the rate of one year per year?"

"Yeah, live a year and get another year, but that's only for newborns *and* it's an average," said Jacob.

"And even so," Jonah continued, "the people have become so averse to any uncertainty that even under the Aggie's nanny state care they've started buying insurance for all kinds of small-stake risks. For instance, many will spend more money to insure some trinket than the trinket is worth. That's called direct risk aversion and it's a kind of behavior that isn't logical. And because they are so focused on living that extra year they are completely oblivious to any opportunity that might carry some risk."

"So much of mankind, except for those in the Solar Federation, have sat on their hands for the past century," said Jacob. "And the Solar Federation is not rich enough to undertake any but carefully considered, reasonable exploration. But still, it has been a golden time for mankind with the help of the Aggies. Most people wouldn't look at it as a loss but a gain."

"And most people wouldn't think about it at all," said Jonah. "So most people wouldn't be prepared should anything upset their comfortable apple cart, would they? Do you remember from your history books the cyber-security disasters?"

"You mean that ancient history, almost two-hundred years ago?"

"Yes, that ancient history taught us one thing. That if we are going to put all our eggs in one basket we had better make sure that basket is secure. When the cyber-attacks took out the electrical grid of the American states on Earth the human suffering was incalculable. A third of the population starved in the first three months. It was almost a year before "normality" was restored. After that you can bet the governments took cyber-security more seriously."

"So what are you saying dad?"

"What I'm saying son is that the same situation exists today. Except this time it is the entire population of Earth and maybe Mars that will be affected by such a catastrophe. Did you ever think what would happen if the Aggies and their computers failed?"

"What do you mean fail? How could they fail?"

"They could fail accidentally or deliberately. There are still a lot of forces on both worlds that would benefit from the collapse of the rule of law. Imagine if cyber-terrorists could implant some viral code into the Aggie systems."

"You think they can?" asked Jacob.

"I don't know but even a slight chance, and I do think there is a slight chance, would lead to economic collapse and misery. Instead of a third of the population of a country dying imagine a third of the population of a world or two."

"The Aggies wouldn't allow that, would they?"

"The Aggies are just programs running on hardware. They have their weaknesses. And remember they have to defend against every intrusion whereas the intruder has to bypass their defenses only once.

"The Aggies have the economies of the whole world inter-meshed and operating at a high degree of efficiency. The problem is that at that level of efficiency there isn't much padding left in the system. If one part of the economy were to falter the other parts would be affected swiftly and drastically. The system is too close-coupled as it exists now. That is why we need to push further out into space without Aggie supervision. To provide a safe place for humanity's future and a way to pick up the pieces if needed."

"You really think that will help if the worse occurs, dad?"

"I don't know for sure, but I do know we can't help if we are caught in the same calamity. Something has to be done, I'm not saying it is all that needs to be done, but it is all that we can do and that's what counts."

3

The Jackson family aboard the *Starfisher* included Jonah and his wife Mia, also their son Jacob and his wife Joanna, Jacob and Joanna's children, John Henry seventeen and Jacob Sanders twenty. Fourteen other crew members and settlers were also aboard the *Starfisher*. The six crew members would stay at Tharsis only long enough for the settlers to become established. That was expected to take two years. The settlement would then have fourteen settlers if no children were born in the meantime.

The *Starfisher* had stowed the settler's small wheel-shaped dwelling that would be spun up upon arrival. This would provide the living quarters, a food production area and enough artificial gravity to maintain human health. The settlers would have with them enough freeze-dried food to last for the first two years. At the end of that time, the aeroponic garden, which was a system to grow plants by applying a mist of water and nutrients to their exposed roots, and the protein production vats, would need to be providing enough food to feed the settlers if they were to stay. The decision would have to be made at that time as to whether or not to abandon the colony. There would only be enough rations left for the eight week trip back to the base orbiting Neptune.

Just as important as food production would be water extraction at Tharsis. It was absolutely essential that water could be produced, the long term success of the colony depended on finding water. Water was not only important for life, but also for the production of hydrogen and oxygen that the dwelling wheel's chemical rockets would need to maintain station. As best as could be determined from a distance of ten astronomical units or nine hundred thirty million miles from Neptune there was water on Tharsis. But even with state of the art equipment the scientists could have made a mistake about water availability on such a small body at such an extreme distance.

Jonah and Jacob were reviewing the latest pictures of Tharsis photographed through the ship's telescope. They were just about to review the spectroscopic data when the all ship alert sounded. Father and son rushed from the forward observation deck down the spine of the ship passing along the way the more slow moving ship bots. They arrived at the revolving main deck where ship's operations was located. This rotating section provided enough artificial gravity to maintain human health over the course of the mission. Also in this section were the sleeping quarters, workout room and galley.

Entering the control room, Jacob and Jonah were alarmed at the level of activity. Ship bots were scurrying in and out, the ship's crew was busy calling out system's status. One after another the Captain called for a status check and the crewman responsible called back nominal. Something was wrong but Jacob and Jonah couldn't make it out.

The litany of call and response continued until Lt. Jensen's readout. Captain Ellis shouted, "Hold it, repeat that again Jensen!"

Jacob knew immediately the problem. Jensen's call out was for the water tanks.

Jensen called his reading again and Captain Ellis let loose a string of impressive expletives followed by a bark at Jensen to shut-off access and depressurize the water tanks with low readings.

Ellis saw Jonah and Jacob in the control room. "Gentlemen," he said. "Meet me in my wardroom." The Captain was already moving towards the exit as he spoke, with the ship recorder bot, Ahab, chasing after him.

"Well gentlemen," said the Captain as Jonah and Jacob entered the room. "We have a serious problem. Clements what's the situation?"

Lt. Commander Clements was the second in command. "Sir, of the ten primary water tanks the hull bots tell us that we have incurred damage to eight. Water loss is estimated to be eighty percent in those eight, we will have an exact number soon. The remaining tanks seem to be functioning but had already been partially emptied due to normal usage."

A string of epithets issued from Captain Ellis which he asked Ahab to strike from the record. He then asked, "What happened Clements?"

"From the octagonal geometry of the tanks it appears that we were hit from the side by some type of fast moving projectiles."

"From the side?"

"Yes sir, the damaged tanks are on the right side of the ship, the two facing outward on that side and then the next two on either side of those two and finally one tank on each side behind those."

"How did the tanks in back get damaged?"

"I'm not sure sir."

"That response is unacceptable Clements, speculate if you can do no better," demanded the Captain.

"Well if I had to speculate, I would say that the projectiles went through the front of the outer tanks and into the ones behind them."

"Clements, do you have any idea the energy it would take to traverse the walls of the first tank and the water and still have the energy to pierce the wall of the next tank?"

"Yes sir. I know the speed of the projectile would have to be enormous."

"You could just about rule out any naturally occurring accelerator," said Jacob. "Nothing I'm aware of in this area of the Solar System could account for the speed required."

"It sounds like whatever it was that pierced the tanks may still be in those back two," said Jonah. "Would it be possible to recover those fragments?"

"Clements?" inquired Captain Ellis.

"I will discuss it with McGraw sir, we can probably rig a hull bot to retrieve them."

"Alright," said the Captain. "Until we find out what hit us we need to come up with an estimate of the effect this incident has on the mission. Clements I want you to work with the chief engineer and the navigator to find us some options concerning our mission goals and whether or not we can still make the original objective. Jonah and Jacob would you please come up with a plan for water conservation that will support the original mission goals?"

"Yes Captain," said Jonah.

"Good, I will expect your preliminary reports this time tomorrow. Thank you gentlemen for your time."

4

Jacob worked on the report overnight. He ran scenarios for one to twelve weeks of water supply on his ANI (Artificial Narrow Intelligence) based assistant usually called and Annie. With the working estimate of the remaining water that Clements had given him Jacob found that the water supply would be depleted sometime between four and six weeks. He would refine his estimates later after the meeting with Captain Ellis. Right now he was going to see his dad and discuss the situation.

"Hi dad," said Jacob as he entered his parent's quarters. "Where's mom?"

"She's working in the kitchen I think son."

"Well I've got some preliminary results from my calculations," said Jacob.

"What have you found?"

"It looks like if we continue usage at the rate we have been since leaving Neptune we've got some four to six weeks of water supply left. That is assuming no problem comes up with the recycling."

"So basically," said Jonah. "We can continue the mission and decelerate into a rendezvous with Tharsis but if we do we had better find water there fast or we are in trouble."

"And I don't know that we have a choice," said Jacob. "There aren't many alternative destinations this far out. And there isn't enough water to make it to a destination that isn't as well researched as Tharsis."

"That will be the Captain's decision but I believe you are right, I think we need also to come up with a water reduction plan that we can present to the Captain."

"Okay dad we have a few hours before the meeting, let's see what we can do."

Jonah didn't respond immediately. "What is it dad?"

"I've been wondering what got us into this mess to begin with. What hit us?"

"I've got an idea about that also," said Jacob. "But let's get the water reduction plan first and then I'll tell you what I'm thinking."

The meeting was attended by Jonah and Jacob and all the crew except for two. Ahab was recording. Captain Ellis opened by saying, "I don't have to tell you all the serious problem we face. We need to make an immediate decision as to how we should proceed with this mission. I want options and I have asked several of you to present your findings on relevant concerns. We will start with Jacob Jackson. I asked Jacob to look into the water situation and its effect on the mission."

"Thank you Captain Ellis, with Lieutenant Commander Clements' input I have run several scenarios for the water situation. I've sent copies to all your Annies but for now, I will only present what I feel is the bottom line. We have enough water left to last us for four to six weeks. You are all probably aware that this is almost exactly the amount of time we will need to decelerate and rendezvous with Tharsis. I don't see any other choicc but . . ."

"Thank you Mr. Jackson," interrupted the Captain. "The information we needed was your water estimate but how we act upon that information will be up to myself as the commanding officer of this vessel."

"Navigator," said the Captain. "Were you aware of Mr. Jackson's water estimate?"

"Yes sir," said Lt. Wilson. "Lt. Commander Clements informed me early this morning."

"So you have had time to come up with the effect it has on our mission and propose alternatives?"

"Yes sir, Mr. Jackson is correct in his estimate if we continue to pursue our original course. We should have enough water to rendezvous with Tharsis. However sir, knowing that you would want all alternatives I have come up with some other destinations."

"Go ahead Lieutenant."

Lieutenant Wilson proceeded to present several alternative destinations. Besides Tharsis, he had also calculated the possibility of returning to the Neptune system. Although this would completely exhaust the water they could request a refitting vessel be dispatched from Neptune when they got close enough.

Another possibility would be diversion to the Terran Federation outpost orbiting Pluto. This would take the least amount of water and the course corrections were rather small at this time. They could arrive there between two and three weeks. Upon arriving at the outpost orbiting Pluto there should be plenty of water left and replenishing the supplies would be possible as well as repairing the tanks. Then the Captain could decide whether to continue the mission to Tharsis or return to Neptune.

"Thank you Lieutenant. You've provided me with alternatives which I always appreciate. Now I would like for Lieutenant Commander Clements to present his findings on exactly what hit us."

"Thank you Captain. Samples of the material that punctured the tanks were acquired by the hull bots. What they returned was assayed by Chief Engineer McGraw and Starman Lewis, it seems to be debris that would be commonly found in an M-type nickel-iron asteroid. The fragments contain heavy iron ore. The density of the fragments and their suspected velocity supplied more than enough energy to puncture the water tanks."

"Where did they come from Lt. Commander?" asked the Captain.

"From the hole alignment between tanks, I would say the source was quite outside the elliptic and inbound into the inner Solar System."

Jacob stirred. "Are you sure Lt. Commander?" he asked.

"Yes Mr. Jackson the Chief and I both concur. But you may study our data if you wish."

"That won't be necessary," said Jacob. "I was just surprised at the direction, I expected more of an orbit in the plane of the solar system."

"That's understandable Mr. Jackson. The Chief and I were both surprised also."

"Okay," said Captain Ellis. "I think I have all the information I need to make a decision as to our next move. I want to thank all of you for your efforts. Gentlemen you are dismissed."

5

Back in the family quarters, Jonah asked his son, "You seem concerned about what you heard in the meeting?"

"I'm concerned that we didn't hear the truth dad. Something about the results Lt. Commander Clements and Chief McGraw came up with doesn't make sense to me."

"What do you mean son?"

"Well unless I learned my orbital mechanics completely wrong, and my Annie also is totally confused, whatever hit us was not in the orbital plane of the solar system."

"But isn't that what the Lt. Commander said?"

"Yes he did say that. But what they were saying doesn't make any sense. The strikes to the water tanks lined up with the orbital plane of the solar system. I know this from reviewing the hull bot data myself. They said the projectiles came from outside the plane."

"That's right," said Jonah. "But you just said that the projectiles couldn't be in the plane of the solar system because of their velocity."

"I know. They couldn't be naturally occurring projectiles because they were moving too fast. See at this distance any orbiting material wouldn't be traveling fast enough and therefore would not have enough energy to do all the damage we witnessed. Maybe the first tank could have been pierced but the orbital energy should have been expended in that tank without enough energy left to pierce the back wall. That is what the design engineers of the *Starfisher* expected."

"So the projectiles weren't naturally occurring. Then the question is where did they come from?"

"The only thing I can think of is that we were fired upon by another spaceship from an extreme distance. Far enough away that they wouldn't be detected. And I would say a ship with an electromagnetic rail-gun. That would explain the velocity and accuracy of the projectiles that hit the water tanks."

"That is incredibly risky, who would have done such a thing?" asked Jonah. "And why?"

"My best guess is a Terran Federation patrol ship. They are the only ones out this far with the necessary weaponry on-board to initiate such an attack. It could have been a ship stationed at their outpost on Pluto."

"But why son?"

"I don't know why. But did you notice that one of the options that Lt. Wilson proposed is docking at the Pluto outpost for repairs? That's not something that would have occurred to me since we should be able to effect the repairs ourselves once we reach Tharsis. And then we can restore our lost water."

"But the Captain has to consider that the advance intelligence about Tharsis could be wrong. We could get there and find that the water we need is non-existent."

"There is a chance that's true," said Jacob. "But it is a small chance and there are other bodies near Tharsis that we would have the time and resources to explore. You know that most of the asteroids in the Kuiper Belt have frozen volatiles such as methane, ammonia *and* water.

"So I think this diversion is deliberate but what I don't understand is why they went through all of this, especially as it was a dangerous ploy, to get us to Pluto?"

"Maybe I can answer that," said Jonah. "The outpost orbiting Pluto is a Terran Federation base and the Federation has found itself playing catch up with the Solar Federation ever since the days of the national breakups on Earth some seventy years ago. They've also seen their influence on Earth diminish. They've seen their influence in space diminish. That is why they've hop-scotched to Pluto, to get some relevance again.

"Now they find that we are going to establish a base in the Kuiper Belt that they won't control. We could essentially make their outpost orbiting Pluto superfluous. But what if they could stop or at least control the settling of the Kuiper Belt? They would be of importance again and it would enhance their influence on Earth and around the Solar System."

"I don't understand."

"What's that son?"

"The Terran Federation is a representative of some of the same governments that support our mission. Yet those governments are allowing this interference?"

"Well support is probably too strong of a word son. They may not be directly interfering but they have no qualms about interfering through their proxy, the Federation."

"Plausible deniability," said Jacob.

"Yes," said Jonah.

It was the next morning and Captain Ellis had gathered together the settlers to tell them his decision.

"I've called you here," said Captain Ellis, "to let you all my decision concerning the future of this mission. As you know we have to make this decision because of the damage to our water supplies. My decision has been guided by this basic point, we have no mission without the necessary water.

“Taking into account this need for water to achieve our eventual goal, which is to deliver you settlers to Tharsis, I believe the mission will be best served by diverting the *Starfisher* to the Terran Federation outpost orbiting Pluto. They've got the necessary resources and tools to repair and resupply this mission. I've already contacted the outpost and told them our needs. They wholeheartedly agreed to help us with our repairs and resources at no cost.

“Any questions?”

Jacob spoke up, “What about other supplies Captain, like food? Will they be able to replenish those also?”

“To a certain extent,” said the Captain seemingly annoyed. “They will be able to help us with all our supplies but we will have to institute some rationing I'm afraid to make sure we meet the mission requirements.”

“I see,” said Jacob. “Thank you Captain.”

“Any other questions?”

No other questions were forthcoming so the Captain dismissed the assembly.

6

Jonah and Jacob talked quietly on the way back to their quarters stopping whenever a ship bot came rolling by.

"They seem to have it all planned," said Jacob.

"Yes son they do but I'm still not sure how many are involved."

"I think Lt. Wilson is involved," said Jacob.

"Maybe."

"What should we do?" asked Jacob.

"I'm not sure. The question is what do they want us to do?"

"Obviously to go along with their mission interference."

"Obviously," said his father. "But I was thinking more about what the end game might be. I think either they are going to want us to agree to founding Tharsis under the umbrella of the Terran Federation or . . ."

"Yes father?"

"Or they do not want Tharsis founded at all and then the question becomes, what happens to us?"

Late the following day Lt. Commander Clements called Jonah and Jacob to his wardroom for a brief meeting.

"Thank you for coming," said the Lieutenant Commander. "I've been tasked by the Captain to come up with the necessary adjustments to the supplies to see that we can complete this mission. Here are my conclusions which I have already shown to the Captain."

He showed Jonah and Jacob his summary, cast from his Annie so all could view.

"As you can see," continued the Lt. Commander, "we will have to make some adjustments, especially in our food supplies. But I believe that with an expansion of our food production centers we can keep these adjustments to a minimum. After conferring with the Captain we were both hoping that you gentlemen might take on the task of expanding the centers."

Jonah briefly looked at the numbers and said, "Of course Lt. Commander my son and I will do our best."

"Oh thank you," said Clements obviously relieved. "We really appreciate your attitude in this matter as we do all the other settlers."

After further discussion of the necessary resources needed to expand the centers, Jonah and Jacob left the Lt. Commander.

"You were quick in agreeing?" questioned Jacob.

"Yes son I was, for a reason. You see the fact that they are interested in reducing the imposition upon us as much as possible tells me that they still have future plans for us. That is good and we must do whatever we can until such time that we can gain the upper hand in negotiations. It is for the safety of ourselves and the rest of the srttlers that we act."

"I understand father," said Jacob admiringly.

The *Starfisher* had made it to the Pluto outpost. In the two weeks since the docking none of the settlers had been allowed aboard the station, supposed security protocol required the quarantine. It was then that the Captain informed Jonah that the station Commander would be coming aboard to discuss the future of the mission with him and Jacob.

The following day station Commander Vasily Bogdonich came aboard the *Starfisher*. He met with the Captain, the Lieutenant Commander and Jonah and Jacob in the Captain's quarters.

Sitting around a small table Commander Bogdonich began, "Captain, Lt. Commander, Mr. Jackson and Jacob Jackson I thank you for attendance. I am sorry that we have had to keep you here on the ship for the past two weeks but it is standard procedure for the station, I hope you understand."

"Of course Commander," said Jonah. "We understand the need for such procedures."

"Thank you Mr. Jackson, we in the Terran Federation welcome you to our advanced outpost. I want to assure you that soon you and the rest of the settlers will be allowed to freely come and go from the station. What I want to discuss with you and your son as representatives of the others is our concerns for completing the mission you are set upon. I can assure you that the Federation fully supports your goals."

"Thank you Commander," said Jacob. "May I ask when we will be able to continue our flight to Tharsis?"

"Yes Mr. Jackson that is the question. Captain Ellis do you have an estimate on the time required to repair the *Starfisher*?"

"Commander Bogdonich we believe we can have the *Starfisher* ready for deep space in a month's time."

"Very good Captain," said Bogdonich. "Now Mr. Jackson, Jonah and Jacob, what we would like for you to do is to continue your expansion of the food growing facility not only on the *Starfisher* but also on the station. In this way, we can be more assured to have the necessary food supplies ready when the *Starfisher* departs. You would of course, have at your disposal as many station bots and men as we can spare."

"Very well Commander," said Jonah. "My son and I and the rest of the settlers will do our best in the time we have. But Commander may I ask you one question?"

"Of course Mr. Jackson."

"A month will not be very much time to expand and increase the food production at the station. I doubt that we will get the benefit of the first crop in just four weeks."

"That may be true, Mr. Jackson. But although the repairs may be finished in a month the departure of the *Starfisher* may be held up until we get that first harvest. And besides, don't you think that it is an equitable trade, you expand the station's food supply while we repair and replenish your ship?"

"I do indeed Commander," said Jonah.

"Alright then," said Bogdonich. "If there are no more questions I suggest we all get to work."

"What gives?" asked Jacob of his father after they had separated from the others.

"Well son I find it curious but an equitable trade of labor."

"What do you mean?"

"I mean I think the *Starfisher* will be ready to leave in a month and will leave at that time."

"But then why are we increasing the food growing capacity of the station?"

"Because we settlers are going to need it to survive at the outpost when the *Starfisher* leaves us behind," said Jonah.

7

"That don't make no sense Jonah," said Lars Stendahl, one of the colonists. "You know we can't build up the infrastructure and get a crop of food in a month."

Jonah had called a meeting of all the colonists.

He replied to Lars, "Well the Commander did say that it might be longer than a month before the *Starfisher* departs. And he did make the point that it was an equitable trade of labor, expanding their food production facilities in return for them helping to repair our ship."

"I still say it's suspicious," said Lars.

"That's as may be," said Jonah. "But I suggest we get to work and do the best we can to show our hosts our gratitude for their help in repairing the *Starfisher*. Are there any more questions?"

Upon hearing none, Jonah dismissed the meeting.

"Are you coming Jonah?" asked his wife Mia. "You go ahead dear I want to speak to Jacob a moment. Jacob if you would come over here."

"Yes father," said Jacob as he came up to Jonah.

"Jacob it is very important that the food supply capability on the station be increased enough to accommodate not only the station personnel but colonists also."

"I know father you've told me about your suspicions."

"Yes I know but I'm afraid it may be hard to motivate the others without letting them know what I suspect. If as I expect, when the *Starfisher* leaves the dock and we find most of the colonists left on the station the food production capacity will be essential to their health and maybe their survival."

"You are saying most of the colonists now father, what do you mean?"

"I think they will take some of us along to manage the food production facilities on the *Starfisher*. I don't think they have enough know-how or manpower otherwise. Anyway, as I was saying, I want you to make sure that the production facilities on the station are expanded and ready by the end of the month. Do whatever you find is necessary to motivate the people, understand son?"

"Yes father."

Jacob had a crew of twelve including himself and four station personnel assigned by the Commander. He divided them into two teams of six each, one headed by himself and one headed by Jonah. Each man in a team had at his disposal a couple of station bots to help. Jacob asked each team to work six hours a shift so that he had at least six people working twelve hours a day for a month. If things went smoothly he had figured this would be sufficient to expand the facilities of the station and start a crop of foodstuff before the month ran out. But it would be close.

To encourage productivity he set up a challenge between the teams. His metrics were square footage of food production facility expanded and square footage of plants planted. Lars and a couple of other colonists would inspect and decide which team had done the best job at the end of the month.

Jacob had been working on the project for several days when one of the station men assigned to his team approached him. "Mr. Jackson?"

"Yes Jack what can I do for you."

"Well I would like to discuss with you something that has bothered me for some time now."

"About the work we're doing?"

"No sir, not directly. It's about conditions on the station."

Jacob waited, then said, "Okay Jack, what do you want to discuss?"

"Mr. Jackson," Jacob interrupted and asked to be called Jacob.

"Okay then, Jacob, what I know that you may not know," he stopped and looked around.

Seeing no one nearby he continued, "Well, you see, we've been under strict rationing on the station for months now. I think that either a mistake was made when the station was designed or we are over the limits when it comes to personnel. What I don't understand is why they've waited until now to do something about it."

"That's interesting Jack. I can't speak to the design issues but let me ask you a question. Is there anyone on the station that has training in agriculture or protein production?"

"No. Many of us are just workers without any specialized knowledge except for what we were taught before we were sent to the station. Of course in engineering and some of the other specialized departments, department heads have some education in biology. At that level, you have to be versed in multiple disciplines to be chosen by the Terran Federation. But I don't think any of their specialties include agriculture."

"Well my dad Jonah has an advanced degree in Agronomy and I have an undergraduate specialization in Agricultural Sciences. So I would say that Commander Bogdonich is just taking advantage of the situation."

"That may be so. But Mr. Jackson, I mean Jacob, don't you think that at least one person on the station should have had a background in agriculture like you or your dad. You all realized on the *Starfisher* that it was important to have that level of expertise aboard, why didn't the Federation?"

"I can't say Jack, maybe they thought that the design would be sufficient if just worked properly."

"Jacob we have gone hungry for months. I can only believe that it was through incompetence, inaction or callous disregard for the welfare of their people that a proper supply of food was relegated to such a low priority. Jacob it's almost criminal."

Jacob and Jonah both had discussions with the men assigned to them from the station personnel. They all felt some disappointment and animosity towards their Federation leaders. Except for the term limits in their contract it was apparent that they might have taken matters into their own hands by now. As it was, any discipline enacted against them only brought greater disdain for the officers and the Federation itself.

One evening Jacob and Jonah were talking about the day's work. Jacob mentioned again a discussion he had with one of the station men.

"I am surprised," began Jacob, "about the animosity he shows towards the Federation officers. That could only have been building over a period of time and hasn't been properly addressed by the leaders. It shows poor leadership, poor planning, a complete lack of regard for their people."

"Well," said Jonah. "We've known for some time that the Terran Federation in many ways is an organization that is underfunded and over-ambitious. Obviously they are trying to stretch their resources and cut costs any way they can.

"That's okay when you are on the surface of a planet. But space is not so forgiving of incompetence or carelessness. The lives of these men were and are being endangered by the Federation, there's no doubt in my mind."

"I think that listening has helped them," said Jacob.

"I do too. It may also help us when the time comes," said Jonah.

8

The month was up and Lars and the other colonists had decided that Jonah's team had done the best job although the choice was close. Both teams were invited to a dinner, to be prepared by the other colonists as a gesture of appreciation for their hard work.

At the dinner, Jack had some news for Jonah.

"Jonah I have some news that is not official yet but I think it will be announced tomorrow. I have heard that the Federation has decided to send the *Starfisher* to Tharsis with a station crew aboard and only a minimum of colonists. The colonists except for those chosen to go will stay behind on the station. I think that is why we were employed to expand the food supply there."

"Yes Jack I suspected that something like that would happen. I expect that you and the other station personnel that helped expand the food supply aboard the station will go and that Jacob and I will go. I think the Federation has learned about the importance of the food supply to missions out here."

"Of course Jonah, I should have known you would have already figured out what was going on. I wish you were in charge of the station, I and most of the other workers would be a lot more comfortable with you in charge. By the way, do you have any idea why they are sending a station crew instead of you colonists?"

"Jack I thank you for your confidence in me. But I don't know everything. I don't know the end game yet."

The dinner finished, the station crew dispersed, and the colonists settled down for the night. Jonah informed Jacob of what Jack had said. They were both confident that their suspicions had been confirmed but also worried that they had not figured out what the Terran Federation was planning.

The next morning a meeting of the colonists was called in the main hall of the station. Upfront were seated the station brass with the recorder bot Ahab. In the front row were the men that had helped Jonah and Jacob with the expansion of the station's food supply.

The station Commander Bogdonich stood. "I thank you all for coming this morning. I want to announce the status of the *Starfisher* mission. We believe we will be ready to launch the mission in no more than two weeks. By arrangement with the Solar Federation, the mission will include ship personnel. It will also include these men you see here in the front row that helped expand the food supplies on the station and four other station men. And we request, although we certainly do not order, that Jonah and Jacob Jackson accompany the mission."

Several colonists raised their voices in protest. Commander Bogdonich tried to quell them. "Let me continue," he said. "Let me continue please." The crowd acquiesced.

"Thank you," said the Commander. "As I was saying we are asking Jonah and Jacob Jackson to accompany the mission voluntarily. The Terran Federation has realized it's mistake in managing the food supplies and is working hard to correct these errors. This is why the top administrators at the Federation have asked me to thank Jonah and Jacob personally for all they have done. And to ask them to continue training the men that have worked with them for the past month along with the new men. We feel that with their help we can correct any shortcomings we have in this area."

Jacob stood and said, "Commander Bogdonich I believe I speak for my son when I say we will accept your request and accompany the mission to Tharsis. But I do want to ask you one thing, what are the Federation's long term plans for colonization there?"

"Well to be frank the Terran Federation has no plans for long term colonization of Tharsis by Federation personnel. The long term goal is still to deliver you settlers. But the Terran Federation has been made aware of the risks such a mission might encounter by *Starfisher* detouring here for repair. That made the Federation a partner and a responsible party for this mission and we believe that we would be negligent to let the other settlers, particularly the women and children, proceed on this mission without first establishing a basis for safety. So the mission has essentially been broken up into two phases.

First, the Federation and *Starfisher* personnel along with you and your son Jacob will scout out Tharsis and if possible prepare a base of operations for future settlement. Then once we are comfortable that the risks have been reduced as much as possible the *Starfisher* will return, refit and carry the other settlers to the base. The Terran Federation believes that this initial reconnaissance will reduce the risk to an acceptable level for the women, children and others."

"Yeah, and what does the Federation get for their efforts to save us," said Lars contemptibly.

"You are Lars Stendahl?"

"That I am."

"Well Mr. Stendahl the Terran Federation does not expect anything. The Jackson's have already been of great assistance and will be of further assistance on the reconnaissance mission. However, if in the future should the colony live up to its aims of establishing a way station and fuel depot then it might show consideration if any Federation ships out that way were serviced at a discount, to be mutually agreed upon with you colonists, of course."

"That's what I thought," said Lars abruptly, then sat down.

"Very well," said the Commander. "Are there any other questions or concerns we should address?"

"Commander," said Jacob. "How long a mission are we planning? I take it to be at least four weeks to Tharsis, has it been decided how long we will stay there?"

"The mission to Tharsis, the stay-over and the return trip should take no more than fourteen weeks."

Jacob's wife Joanna squeezed his arm tightly.

9

Preparations had gone well, the *Starfisher* left Pluto Station on time and was well on it's way to Tharsis without incident. The *Starfisher* was adjusting its velocity to "catch up" to Tharsis and altering its orbital inclination to match.

It wasn't long until Lt. Commander Blyton, sent by Bogdonich to watch over the station men, established his supremacy over them, and again it didn't take long until his orders incensed the men. Just as on the station, he had a way of demeaning a man even while praising him. And it wasn't long until Jack and the other station men were complaining to Jonah as bitterly as before.

"Jonah, may I speak with you," said Jack.

"Of course Jack what is on your mind?"

"Jonah, Lt. Commander Blyton has ordered rationing again. At least for us station men. I don't understand it. You know the food situation, do we need to ration?"

"I don't think so Jack. According to my calculations, we should have plenty of food for the entire mission. But perhaps the Lt. Commander is just being overly careful."

"Maybe. But I think it is just his way of lording it over us. Just like on the station. He and the Commander were always coming up with some goals that we had to meet. Work capacity, rationing, watch duties, as if we were always in danger or always at war. It just keeps the men off balance and disgruntled. Such continuous harassment doesn't lead to a man's best performance, I can tell you that."

"I understand. Maybe I will speak with the Lt. Commander and assure him that the food supplies are abundant and robust and there really is no need for any rationing on the ship."

"Thanks Jonah, I knew me and the other men could depend on you to speak up for us."

Jonah was back from meeting with the Lt. Commander.

"How did it go dad?" asked Jacob.

"Not good son. I tried to present my findings on the food supply to the Lt. Commander but he was completely uninterested. I'm afraid it got worse. He accused me of interfering with the chain of command. I tried to point out that I was just presenting my report but dropped my protestations and left as he seemed completely unreasonable on the subject."

"I don't understand dad, what is going on?"

"I'm not sure son but I'm guessing that the animosity that has built up between the station brass and the workers is being carried over into this mission. The Lt. Commander was Commander Bogdonich's enforcer on the station. And the Lt. Commander seems intent on letting these men know that he is still the enforcer."

"What a mess," said Jacob. "That might work planet-side or even on the station but here in these tight quarters of the *Starfisher* I worry that the animosity might explode into action and reaction."

"That's a succinct way to put it son, and I think you are right to be worried."

It wasn't long until the explosion.

Jacob was on his way to aeroponics when he heard someone shouting. Turning a corner he saw Lt. Commander Blyton dressing down Jack Loring.

“Loring,” shouted the Lt. Commander. “You are a disgrace! You've been late for duty almost every day since we left the station! I'm tired of your complaining. You will report to Captain Ellis and he will confine you to your quarters until such time as I decide what your punishment will be. Do you understand!”

“Understand, my punishment!” shouted Loring visibly shaking. “I'll tell you what my punishment should be, nothing! That's right, I've already been punished for the past two years. Joining this ragged, sorry outfit with incompetents such as yourself in command. I'll tell you what my punishment should be, nothing! You can take your officer's airs and shove 'em because you ain't going to punish me!”

Jacob hurried to get to the men but before he could the Lt. Commander had asserted himself. Loring stepped back and took one swing which floored the Lt. Commander. He went down and didn't move.

“Jack,” shouted Jacob as he ran to the man's side. “I wish you hadn't done that. That is insubordination and punishable by imprisonment.”

“Well they will have to catch me before they can inflict their punishment. And that ain't going to be easy I tell you,” said Loring who took off down the hall.

“Wait!” yelled Jacob. But Loring was gone. Jacob bent down to help the Lt. Commander.

“Lieutenant,” Jacob said as he shook the man.

“Lieutenant, can you hear me?”

The Lt. Commander slowly stirred. He looked groggily at Jacob.

"Where is he?" he asked.

"Loring? He's gone."

"Help me up. That man must be arrested and confined to quarters. Help me get to Captain Ellis, he can deputize some of his men to round up Loring. You saw what happened didn't you? You are an eye witness to this crime."

Jacob had gotten Blyton to Captain Ellis' quarters. Captain Ellis was listening to Blyton's story.

Blyton said, "I request that you deputize some of your men Captain Ellis and arrest Jack Loring."

"Lt. Commander," said Ellis. "I have six men and double that number of bots helping me pilot this ship. All the men have multiple duties. Even if I could spare two of these men to do as you wish they would probably not only face Jack Loring but also the rest of your men from the station. I think before we go off and escalate this unfortunate incident we need to find out where the rest of the men stand on this. If they are against arresting Loring I don't see how we can do it. Not without posing a severe risk to this mission."

"That is completely unacceptable Captain and I will include your response in my report to the station. You can expect a complaint filed by the Terran Federation with your Solar Federation," said Blyton as he stormed off.

10

"Jonah, Jacob thank you both for coming," said Captain Ellis at the meeting he had arranged after Captain Blyton's threats. "No doubt you know why I've called you here. I've been placed in an awkward position by Lt. Commander Blyton. He is demanding that I arrest the man Loring and any others that might stand with him. I need your counsel please."

"Captain, my son has filled me in on the unfortunate incident," said Jonah. "I think you have been placed in the middle of a situation that has been brewing for some time between those men and the Lt. Commander. He was wrong to ask you to intercede, he should have handled the situation himself."

"Jonah I'm glad you feel that way. That's what I thought. Those are his men, the problems are his making. I've got my hands full running this ship. I hate to ask you, but can you help as a negotiator between the aggrieved parties. I know that you have the respect of the station men and I suspect that you also have Lt. Commander Blyton's, although he would be the last to admit it."

"Captain we would be pleased to help out in this situation."

Jonah sent Jacob to call the station men to a meeting on the lower deck of the aeroponic's area. The men came into the area looking behind them. They acknowledged Jonah but did not speak. When all were present Jonah spoke.

"Thank you all for coming. I have been asked by Captain Ellis to serve as a liaison between you men and the Captain. He is interested in knowing your grievances and hopes that he can address them. Mr. Loring would you begin, will you tell me what happened between you and the Lt. Commander please."

"Mr. Jackson the Lt. Commander acted belligerently and aggressively towards me. He was the instigator of the confrontation, I was the target."

"I understand Jack but if you don't mind, may I ask why you think he was so aggressive. I mean, is there any background to the problem?"

"Jonah, the Lt. Commander has been riding our backs since we came aboard Pluto Station. You know from your work in aeroponics that they have incompetently handled the station since its establishment. But they absolutely refused to admit to any problems they may are responsible for and instead blame the men trying to do a job under the worse of conditions. Speaking for myself and the rest of the men we should have revolted long ago, it is a measure of our dedication to our tasks that we have allowed this to go on for so long."

Almost in unison the rest of the men were yelling that Loring was telling the truth. Jonah signaled for calm.

"Thank you," said Jonah as the men became silent. "So this breakdown has been building for some time, I see. Then it's not likely that this incident can be papered over with some concessions from both sides. We are going to have to make a more fundamental change in the relationship. Thank you for coming I will let you know as soon as possible my proposal for a resolution."

As the men drifted away Jonah said to Jacob, "Let's go see the Lt. Commander and get his side of the story."

They found the Lt. Commander in his quarters, he seemed composed although the bruise on the side of his face was readily apparent.

After being seated Jonah began, "Lt. Commander we are here to get your side of the incident with Jack Loring."

"I don't understand. Hasn't that man been arrested yet?" demanded Blyton.

"Lt. Commander you are aware that the Captain does not have the resources to facilitate such an arrest," said Jacob.

"I thought perhaps he had enlisted you two."

"Well, he has enlisted us in a way but not in the way you apparently expected. He has asked us to look into the matter and hopefully find a resolution between the parties that does not require a criminal inquiry."

Blyton was about to interrupt but Jonah continued. "We hope that justice may be done on all sides. That is why we need your side of the incident if you would indulge us."

"That man Loring is the biggest goof off on the station. He is constantly late for his assignments, leaves early if I don't watch him and worse of all affects the morale of each and every man he works with. I have been patient with him for two years. I have discussed the matter with him, I have had him talk with the station psychologist, I have offered him incentives to work, I have reprimanded him, I have done everything in my power and I think in a measured way to try to instill in him a work ethic. This mission is critical to the Terran Federation and I am not going to see it fail because of one man, Mr. Loring."

"So there is a long history between you and this Loring. I've no doubt what you say Lt. Commander, Jacob observed the same behavior when he was helping him in aeroponics. And I understand how one man can negatively influence the rest."

"Good, so you two can testify to what you've seen at the court-martial."

"Lt. Commander," said Jonah. "You don't seem to understand. The government on this ship, Captain Ellis, does not see fit to take this incident to court. He wants it settled and as soon as possible."

"Jonah, I will call the station and talk to the Commander, he will, I'm sure insist that the man be placed under arrest until we can try him."

"Lt. Commander you do realize that we are still a long time from returning you and the other men to the station. The Captain is adamant that he will not be responsible for a prisoner that long. More than that, he needs every man performing his duties to the best of his ability. You, of all people, should know that on a space station or spaceship there is simply no room for this kind of drama. We must get beyond this and we must get beyond this now or this mission is in jeopardy."

Blyton looked down for a moment and then said, "You are right Jonah, what do you suggest?"

Just then an all ship alert came blaring through the corridors. "Attention all *Starfisher* personnel, attention all *Starfisher* personnel, assemble on Command deck for further instructions immediately."

"What could that be about?" asked Jacob.

"I don't know but let's follow the Lt. Commander and find out," said his father.

The Lt. Commander was already out the door.

11

By the time Jonah and Jacob had chased the Lt. Commander to the Command deck, all the other *Starfisher* personnel were there except for the Chief Engineer.

"Jonah and Jacob I did not call for you but you are welcome," began Captain Ellis. "It seems that we have a mutiny underway." The men tensed. "The station personnel have blockaded aeroponics and seem to have taken the chief engineer as hostage. The Chief has called me and let me know the demands. It seems the station personnel want us to take them immediately back to Neptune and from there the *Starfisher* is to be refitted, to carry them to Mars. They have embargoed our food supply. We, the *Starfisher* personnel and settlers, have enough food for three days. At that time we will need replenishment from the stores or aeroponics. I've called this meeting for an open discussion as to what our course of action should be."

"We should take them out," said the Lt. Commander. "This is mutiny and should not be allowed to stand!"

"Okay Lt. Commander," said the Captain. "We have your vote. Anyone else?"

"Let me talk to them," said Jonah. "Maybe I can reason with them. Get them to release the Chief and open up aeroponics."

"Anyone else?" asked the Captain.

After a moment he said, "Lt. Commander I think I will have to go with Jonah's suggestion."

"But Captain," began the Lt. Commander.

"Please Lieutenant Commander," said Captain Ellis holding up his hand.

"Jonah use your Annie to stay in touch and try to keep me updated on the hour. Thank you, that is all."

Jonah, Jacob and the bot Ahab, by order of the Captain, were on their way to aeroponics when Jonah felt the lurch. It wasn't severe but it was noticeable.

Ahab spoke, "Your attention, please, I believe we have a malfunction with the ship. Perhaps we should turn back."

In the zero-gravity of the ship's spine, Jonah found himself constantly pushing away from the corridor wall. Something was changing the heading of the *Starfisher*, there wasn't any doubt.

"Don't worry Ahab, I'm sure it is safe to continue," said Jonah.

They continued down to aeroponics stopping at the hatch, now sealed from the inside. Jonah used the intercom.

"Hello aeroponics," he said. "This is Jonah and Jacob Jackson. We are here to discuss terms with you, Captain Ellis has sent us."

There was quiet for a few minutes. Jonah was just about to call again when he heard the hatch opening. One of the station men, with a weapon in his hand, motioned them inside and closed the hatch immediately.

"What's up with the bot?" he said.

"The Captain asked us to bring him as his personal representative," said Jacob.

"Huh, this way."

Aeroponics was not completely without gravity. It was found that the plants did better when there was a gravitational orientation and the water to the plants was much easier to manage. But the gravity generated by the slowly spinning segment was very small and even here Jonah thought he could feel the inertial force of the turning ship.

"Do you feel something odd about the ship's orientation?" he asked the station man. The man did not answer but motioned him to follow.

Aeroponics was, in a way, Jonah's favorite part of the ship. Though deep in the bowels of the spinning wheel the brightly lit green plants were very welcoming. His mood always lifted when he saw the plants growing. But now he saw a section bereft of green and was immediately disturbed.

"What happened here?" asked Jonah. The station man looked but didn't answer.

Finally, they arrived at aeroponic control where the rest of the men along with the chief engineer were assembled.

"Welcome Jonah," said Jack Loring. "You too Jacob. I guess you've come to discuss the situation? But why did you bring him?" Loring was pointing towards Ahab.

"Ahab is here at the request of the Captain, and yes Jack, we are here to discuss the situation," said Jonah. "I've been sent by the Captain to see if we can't work something out. Get the *Starfisher* back on track."

"Well it doesn't matter," said Loring gesturing towards Ahab. "We will soon be in control of even him."

Turning to Jonah he said, "Jonah I would love to accommodate you, more than any man I know, but you are a little too late. We have already decided the future of the *Starfisher* and I'm afraid your expedition to Tharsis. We've decided that the *Starfisher* needs to return to Pluto Station. And once there we are determined to settle with the station leadership."

"But you told the Captain you wanted to be taken back to Neptune and what do you mean 'settle'?"

"A little bit of misdirection Jonah to keep the Captain off guard. And as far as settle, the Terran Federation owes us Jonah, they owe us a lot. We plan on collecting. Control of the station will do for now. If it is not turned over to us we will use the *Starfisher* to take it."

"How will the *Starfisher* take the station? The ship has no weapons but is basically a transport."

"Jonah, weapons are in the eye of the beholder. The *Starfisher* has some fine weapons that can be used against a target such as Pluto Station with good effect. When a man needs a weapon he starts with his hands and we have more than enough of them."

"But the *Starfisher*, Captain Ellis will not allow this."

"The Captain will have no choice. Perhaps you noticed the slight difficulty in maintaining your forward motion as you made your way to aeroponics?"

Jonah nodded.

"That was an after effect of our gaining control of guidance. We are turning the ship slowly and placing it on a heading back to the station. Of course the bridge is doing all they can to block our efforts but we are getting better at it all the time. We already control all communications off ship."

"But what do you hope to accomplish by attacking the station? Why go back there, you could be back at Neptune and finished with the Federation."

"We, me and the other men here, have unfinished business at the station. If we go back home the Commander of the station gets a pass. The

Federation will blame it all on the Lt. Commander here on board the *Starfisher* for failing to keep us under control. That is how Commander Bogdonich has avoided the blame so far. We intend to show the Terran Federation that he, and he alone, is to blame for the failure of this mission as well as their precious station."

"While seeking revenge dig two graves," said Ahab as the men turned to look at him. "So someone said," the bot added.

"Ahab's right," said Jonah. "Revenge is a tricky thing to get right. It rarely ends up the way you expect. I would urge you to reconsider Jack. I can assure you that if you will trust me you will have justice. If I fail then you can take your revenge. Let me contact the Captain, he requested that I call in on the hour and it's almost twice that since Jacob and I started down here."

"Jonah you are asking a lot," said Loring.

There was a shout from the hatch area. Then silence.

12

The station men started running towards the sound. Jonah noticed they had drawn weapons from their work clothes, he wasn't sure where they could have gotten them. Loring motioned for Jonah and Jacob to sit next to the Chief Engineer.

"Well Jonah looks like the Captain has made a decision. Your services are no longer needed, if they ever were," said Loring.

"What do you mean?"

"I mean the Captain used you as a decoy to distract us while he set up his little surprise party. I don't blame you Jonah, although I wouldn't have believed you were that gullible."

Jonah said nothing as more shouts were heard. A modern fight with handguns was nothing like in the past. The guns were almost silent. The projectiles were intelligent enough to guide themselves once a target was marked. They were also intelligent enough not to breach the hull of ships but only human targets unless programmed otherwise. So the only way that Jonah could judge the disposition of the battle was when someone shouted.

Out of the dark came a projectile unseen and unheard. The Captain's recorder bot Ahab rocked backward as metal shredded and flew. Jacob upon reaching the bot declared he was off-line, probably permanently.

Jonah knew that one of the station men had to have programmed his weapon to take out the bot.

Another of the station men returned to inform Loring that they were under attack by the ship's crew. A station man had been injured but the others were able to hold off the attackers.

Loring said, "Okay Sam, what I want you to do is get Glassen and work on the power shutdown scenario we've discussed, the rest of the men can hold out until the Captain realizes his mistake and calls off this idiot attack."

The man ran to get Glassen.

Loring turned to Jonah, "Jonah what has happened is that the Captain is a hundred years behind in his thinking. Maybe you can use sidearms if you have overwhelming control of your environment but if you don't, maybe you shouldn't force your enemies hand."

"What are you going to do Jack?"

"We are going to wrest control of the *Starfisher* from the Captain from down here. Command will be superfluous once we are finished and the Captain will either surrender or die."

The *Starfisher* groaned, there was a definite turning motion, now more noticeable. The men returned from the hatch area.

"We left Sid and Darby at the door," said one of the men. "We have placed the station bots in front of the hatch as obstacles, the Captain and his men will have to deal with the bots as we are shooting at them. Joe has been wounded."

The wounded man looked pale, two station men were laying him on the deck.

Jacob said, "Get me the medic kit and let me treat him."

"Yes Jack," said Jonah. "Jacob has training."

While Jacob was treating the injured man Jonah and Loring talked.

"It won't be long," said Loring. "Power and life support are being turned off to all decks but aeroponics. Jonah I need you to go out the other hatch and get your people and bring them here. Captain Ellis hasn't enough men to cover both hatches. Once you and the other colonists are here Captain Ellis and his crew will either surrender and seek shelter here or die."

Jonah didn't answer he was on his way to the other settlers.

"Quick," said Jonah upon seeing his wife. "Grab our emergency kit and help me round up the rest of the colonists."

"What's wrong Jonah?"

"You hear that?"

"No, I don't hear anything."

"That's the problem, life support has stopped. You don't hear anything because the fans are dead. Power to lights and other systems will be next. We need to be on our way to aeroponics by then. I'll explain the rest later."

Jonah rushed away to tell the others, his wife sought out their emergency kit and met him in the hall where the rest of the settlers had gathered. They started the trek to aeroponics.

Jonah and the others had been in aeroponics for several hours. They were making themselves comfortable and gathering a meal when shouts came from the hatch area.

Shortly the Captain and the rest of his crew walked in. They had their spacesuits on with helmets under their arms.

The Captain addressed Loring, “Loring what you have done is equivalent to mutiny. You know that don't you? And I see,” as he pointed toward Ahab, “you have also destroyed Solar Federation property.”

“Whatever you say Captain,” said Loring. “But a man has to recognize authority before he can mutiny against it doesn't he? And me and the rest of the station men do not recognize such authority. However, we welcome you as our guests provided you have turned over all your arms.”

“We have surrendered to your men all our arms I assure you of that Loring.”

“Very well make yourselves comfortable. I believe the settlers are preparing a meal. I'm sure they wouldn't mind sharing with you and your men,” said Loring as he turned away to talk to the man that had unarmed the Captain and crew.

“Jonah,” said Captain Ellis as they were eating their meal together, “do you know his end game?”

“Loring and the rest of the men expect to take over Pluto Station.”

“You're joking. And how do they expect to do that with the few weapons they have?”

“It's true they only have a few sidearms but they have something else as you found out yourself. They know how the technology works. I expect they plan to take over the station the same way they took over the *Starfisher.*”

"I don't believe it."

"That's as may be Captain but that is their plan. Now if I may ask you a question?"

"Yes?"

"Everything that has happened so far on this mission points to collusion between the Terran Federation and one or more of you men. You care to tell me which ones?"

The Captain looked at Jonah a moment, he was just about to protest but thought better of it.

"All of us Jonah."

13

Station Commander Bogdonich called the meeting to order. He called on Lieutenant Vasilikov to present his results.

Vasilikov began, "Commander we have run a full diagnostics in communications. The hull bots report no physical problems with the antenna. There doesn't appear to be any malfunction here at the station. We believe that the problem must lie with the *Starfisher*."

Bogdonich spoke up, "Okay Lieutenant. Then it is apparent that we will not find out the *Starfisher's* status through communications. I need suggestions on how to determine that status as soon as possible."

There was quiet. Vasilikov said, "Commander I don't believe we have any way of determining the status of the *Starfisher* at the probable distance they have traveled from the station."

"So none of you has any ideas?" asked Bogdonich. After almost a minute of silence in which the Commander piercingly surveyed each man in the room.

These officers are supposed to be the best the Terran Federation has to offer, thought the Commander.

Bogdonich finally said, "It seems we haven't had any ideas since the station men left on the *Starfisher*." After letting that sink in he said, "All of you are dismissed!"

Vasilikov approached him but before he could speak the Commander turned away and said, "All of you get out now!"

The *Starfisher* was only a week out from Pluto Station when Loring called for Jonah to come to him.

"Come in Jonah," said Loring. "Have a seat."

"Hello Jack. How are you?"

"I'm fine Jonah, thank you. I wanted to discuss something with you that I have been thinking about since you and I first talked on the station. Actually I've been feeling guilty for not telling you."

"What is it Jack?"

"You know Jonah that I and the rest of the men respect you a great deal. You are the only person since we signed up for Pluto Station that has treated us like human beings and not just station machinery. That is why I think you should know about the plans the Terran Federation and some in the Solar Federation have for this mission."

"Plans?"

"Yes Jonah. You see these people wanted to take Tharsis away from you. They had plans for the Lt. Commander and us station men along with the *Starfisher* crew to establish a base of operations on Tharsis. You and the other settlers were to be forced to return to Neptune on the *Starfisher*. The Terran Federation would claim that the conditions found on Tharsis made it unsuitable for settlers, especially women and children. Some in the Solar Federation might protest but would be expected to eventually acquiesce. I'm sorry Jonah."

"I see, is that why you and the other men took over the *Starfisher*?"

"I'll admit it is one of the reasons Jonah. No doubt our grievances with The Terran Federation had something to do with it too. But the treachery exhibited towards you and the other settlers may have been the catalyst, the last straw for most of the men and certainly for me."

"Thank you Jack for telling me. But I have to say that even though some in both Federations have been insincere in their dealings with us and with you, I wish you and the men would turn over the *Starfisher* to Captain Ellis. You are throwing away your future, you will be outlawed by all the worlds. You will be running from the authorities for the rest of your lives. It isn't any way to live Jack."

"I appreciate your concern Jonah but here's my reply. By not providing adequate sustenance the Terran Federation broke its contract with me and the men, showing no concern for our physical welfare. They showed their contempt for our public reputation by involving us in this ridiculous plot to take Tharsis from you. They are totally and completely without any sense of propriety. We will stand up to them now by refusing to cooperate with their schemes. Their arrogance will eventually be clear for all to see and others will join us in our resistance."

"That is probably true Jack. But that may take some time."

"We can wait Jonah, we only hope it will occur in our lifetimes."

Jonah continued to talk with Jack during the entire flight back to Pluto Station. Both trying to convince the other to compromise.

Commander Bogdonich had ordered an around the clock long-range monitoring for spacecraft from the last known heading of the *Starfisher*. He expected that if the ship had turned back, its trajectory inbound would be much the same as that outbound. But that meant that the monitoring only included a small patch of space in that direction. Any maneuvering that took the *Starfisher* outside that patch essentially made it invisible to the station's long-range monitoring and that is what Jack Loring had ordered.

The *Starfisher* would not be noticeable by the station until it was upon it. At any rate, close enough for the station men aboard the *Starfisher* to implement their plan to defeat the station's defenses before they were ever brought to bear on the ship.

Bogdonich had just retired to his quarters when the alarms went off. He reached for the comm-link and called the on-duty officer. Before the duty officer could respond the link went dead. The Commander was irritated. Then the lights went out, the quiet hum of the circulation fans stopped next. Now the Commander was starting to seethe. But when the alarm stopped with an uncharacteristic failing moan the Commander was surprised. Such a massive failure of systems was impossible. He used his Annie as a flashlight and headed for the command deck.

It took Commander Bogdonich much longer than he expected to get to command. Station bots immobile and in the way, none of the automatic doors, none of the ladder tows, nothing working. The darkness was difficult to penetrate in places. On the command deck, Bogdonich found his crew reduced to bumping about under the soft glow of emergency lamps.

The duty officer immediately upon seeing Bogdonich began a status report.

"Sir," he said. "We have a massive failure mode. Every system on the station is down as far as we can tell. The engineers are stumped. We have only a single channel of off-station communications available. And that is only powered by the lowest level power source. Not more than docking distance is achievable."

Commander Bogdonich stuttered, "It doesn't ma-make sense. How, how can we have an external radio link working but nothing within the station? I couldn't even call up here on the comm-link. I won't sit here deaf, dumb and blind mister. You, you tell the engineers I want power back now!"

"Yes Commander," said the duty officer as he rushed off towards engineering.

The Commander stood there fuming but beginning to fear the magnitude of the emergency he was facing. His mind was racing, but racing in circles. He felt like rushing to engineering. He felt like crawling back into his bunk in his darkened quarters. Just then the radio crackled and the voice of Jack Loring was heard.

"Pluto Station this is Jack Loring aboard the *Starfisher*. Let me speak with Commander Bogdonich."

Bogdonich was stunned. He didn't move immediately to the communications station. The communications officer motioned to the Commander to take the mic.

"Pluto Station can you read me?"

"Just a moment Mr. Loring," said the communications officer, "the Commander is on his way."

Finally, the Commander moved to the comm station and took the mic. "Th-This is Commander Bogdonich," he said.

"Commander, I have complete control of your station. I am going to prove this to you by having the lighting on the command deck restored at this time."

The lights came on, Bogdonich shielded his eyes.

"Commander, are your lights now on?"

"Yes Loring," replied Bogdonich reluctantly.

"Okay Commander I think you now know what we could do to you and the men on the station if we wished. But I've been talking to Jonah Jackson and he has persuaded me that to continue on this course is not the best thing for me and the rest of the station men aboard *Starfisher*. Instead of making you pay for your past transgressions against us we are going to move on with our lives. Jonah has convinced us that revenge against you would not serve our best interests.

"So, after dropping off the Lt. Commander and Captain Ellis and his men, and picking up the other station men that hired in with us, we plan on taking Jonah and the other settlers to Tharsis. Then me and the rest of the men will take the *Starfisher* to wherever we wish. The *Starfisher* is payment for the remainder of our contract. The Solar Federation and the Terran Federation can work it out, we don't care. Captain Ellis and his men will transfer to the station soon. We will restore the station's normal operation when we have removed the *Starfisher* to a safe distance. That is all Commander."

"Wait!" cried Commander Bogdonich into the mic. "Yo-you can't do that, Tharsis belongs to the Federation, I, I mean..." He stopped, realizing his mistake. He keyed the mic then released it, then sat down. The Commander looked around the deck as if he were searching for someone he might know. Then he put his head in his hands.

"You heard that Jonah! The fool gave it away. I told you the whole mission was a front to further the aims of the Federation."

"I heard," said Jonah walking towards Loring. "And we must be careful not to repeat their arrogance. I urge you to join me in a declaration of our right to proceed as we planned. I also would urge you and all the other men to reconsider the confiscation of the *Starfisher,* though you certainly have reason.

"We could use you men to help establish the settlement at Tharsis. Once settled I think you'll find the future of operations there to be very profitable. No one but the settlers and the leaders of the Solar Federation knows this, but the station we are establishing is just a first in a series of stations to provide engineering support for the Star-Way. Do you know what that is Jack?"

Loring looked startled. He said, “Yeah, I've heard of it. A laser-driven highway to the stars.”

“That's right. The Star-Way that has been a dream for so long is about to become a reality. Just think, sailing ships propelled by light rays between the stars. Eventually a whole network of Star-Ways taking mankind interstellar. Let the Terran Federation have one small solar system if they so desire, we will have the stars.

“This is the beginning Jack and you and the rest of the men could be a part of that beginning. And if you join us you will be entitled to the same consideration as the rest of the settlerts. You will be treated the same under the law which you will assist in defining and rendering. You will have full citizenship of Tharsis settlement.

“If you choose we can send the *Starfisher* back to Pluto Station on automatic after we're established at Tharsis and the Solar Federation can retrieve it at its convenience.”

"But what about the traitors in your own Federation?"

"They'll be rooted out once I send in my report. Join us Jack."

“You've given me and the men something to think about Jonah. Let's get the *Starfisher* on her way to Tharsis first and then the men and I will give you our answer.”

Jonah smiled.

AFTERWORD

This story only mentions the Star Way, the next novella, *The Cloud,* and the following short novel, *First Interstellar,* cover it more completely.

ABOUT THE AUTHOR

D.W. Patterson lives in the USA with his beautiful wife Sarah. He studied physics and read classic science fiction in college and then worked for many years as an electronic design engineer.

Now he's trying to write stories like the ones he once loved. See his website dwpatterson.com for more information.

Hard Science Fiction – Old School.

Also By This Author:

The Future Chron Universe:

To date the Future Chron Universe has:

51 Amazon Top 100's

(15 in the Top 10)

In chronological order.

Volume numbers indicate Universe order.

Book numbers indicate Series order.

From The Earth Series

(Novellas except where noted):

Volume 1, Book 1 – *Whatsoever You Do*

Volume 2, Book 2 – *War Through The Pines*

Volume 3, Book 3 – *Vigilance*

Volume 4, Book 4 – *To Tend And Watch Over*

Volume 5, Book 5 – *Union*

Volume 6, Book 6 – *Circle Of Retribution*

Volume 7, Book 7 – *Freedom From Want*

Volume 8, Book 8 – *Break Up*

Volume 9, Book 9 – *Kuiper Station*

Volume 10, Book 10 – *The Cloud*

Volume 11, Book 11 – *First Interstellar* – A Short Novel

Wormhole Series

(Novels):

Volume 12, Book 1 – *Mach's Metric*

Volume 13, Book 2 – *Mach's Mission*

Open Space Series

(Short Stories):

Volume 14, Book 1 – *Open Space*

Volume 15, Book 2 – *The Old World*

Volume 16, Book 3 – *Insurrect*

Volume 17, Book 4 – *Second Beam*

Volume 18, Book 5 – *All For One*

Volume 19, Book 6 – *One For All*

Volume 20, Book 7 – *Shotgun*

Volume 21, Book 8 – *Allison*

To The Stars Series

(Novellas):

Volume 22, Book 1 – *First One Hundred*

Volume 23, Book 2 – *First Dark Ages*

Volume 24, Book 3 – *Second One Hundred*

Volume 25, Book 4 – *Second Dark Ages*

Volume 26, Book 5 – *Path Of The Long March*

Wormhole Series

(Novel):

Volume 27, Book 3 – *Mach's Legacy*

Robot Series

(Novels):

Volume 28, Book 1 – *Spin-Two*

Volume 29, Book 2 – *Robot Planet*

Volume 30, Book 3 – *The Lattice Of Space*

Time Series

(Novels):

Volume 31, Book 1 – *Time Wars*

Volume 32, Book 2 – *Time's End*

Volume 33, Book 3 – *Frozen Time*

The Remembered Earth Universse:

To date the Remembered Earth Universe has:

8 Amazon Top 100's

Cislunar Series

(Short Stories):

Volume 1, Book 1 – *US Tugs*

Volume 2, Book 2 – *Prototype*

Volume 3, Book 3 – *L1 Or Bust*

Volume 4, Book 4 – *Guidance Box*

Volume 5, Book 5 – *Air Brakes*

Volume 6, Book 6 – *View Point*

Volume 7, Book 7 – *Space Truck*

Volume 8, Book 8 – *Dark Side* – *In Progress*

The Manifold Earth Universe:

Volume 1, Book 1 – *The Realm* – *In Progress*

Don't miss out!

Don't miss out!

Visit the website below and you can sign up to receive emails whenever D.W. Patterson publishes a new book. There's no charge and no obligation.

https://books2read.com/r/B-A-DPWE-FXFJC

BOOKS 2 READ

Connecting independent readers to independent writers.

www.ingramcontent.com/pod-product-compliance
Lightning Source LLC
LaVergne TN
LVHW010501160826
845677LV00012B/2598

9798223537281